Rachel has Eczema

A DOCTOR SPOT CASE BOOK

For Shauni

First published in the UK in 2003 by
Red Kite Books, an imprint of Haldane Mason Ltd
PO Box 34196, London NW10 3YB
email: info@haldanemason.com

ISBN 1-902463-92-7

A HALDANE MASON BOOK

Colour reproduction by Smart Solutions Ltd, UK

Printed in the UAE

Please note:
The information presented in this book is intended as a support to
professional advice and care. It is not a substitute for medical diagnosis or
treatment. Always notify and consult your doctor if your child is ill.

"The Patients Association recognize the need for literature on children's
health that is educational and enjoyable for both the child and parent.
We welcome the publication of this Dr Spot Case Book."

Rachel has Eczema

Jenny Leigh

Illustrated by Woody Fox

ReD KiTE

Name: Rachel Rhino

Age: 4

Sex: Girl

Case Notes: Rachel had very dry, sore skin which itched so much that she just had to scratch! She was feeling very sorry for herself when her mother brought her to see me.

Doctor R Spot

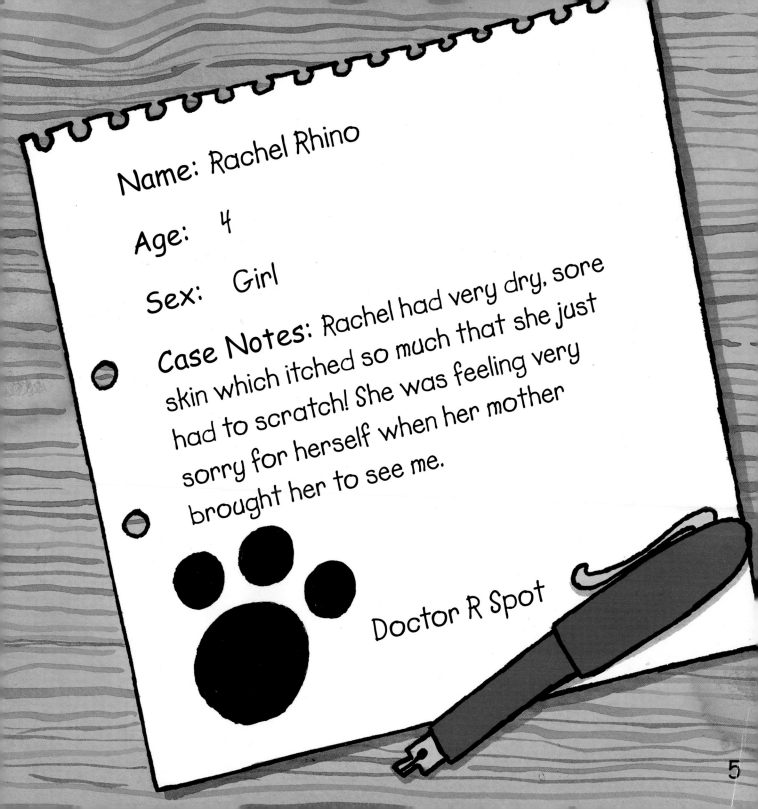

Mr and Mrs Frog were making lunch for their new neighbours, the Rhinoceros family. Mrs Rhino had moved into the house next door with her children, Ronnie and Rachel. *Brrrring*! went the doorbell.

"Franklin!" called Mr Frog. "The Rhinos are here." Franklin hopped downstairs to greet his guests.

"Hello," he said. "You must be Ronnie. Do you want to go and play in the garden?"

"Great," said Ronnie. "What shall we play?"

"I've got a new set of quoits," said Franklin. He eyed Ronnie's long pointy horn, which was just perfect for catching the rope circles!

The two boys ran into the garden.

"And this is Rachel," said Mrs Rhino, trying to pull her daughter out from behind her.

"Hello, Rachel," said Mrs Frog, popping her head round Mrs Rhino. Rachel looked up and Mrs Frog was surprised to see that her face looked all red and sore.

"Oh my!" she exclaimed. "You do look very . . . hot," she finished.

"Rachel has a skin problem," sighed Mrs Rhino.

"Poor dear," said Mrs Frog kindly. "Would you like to go and play with the boys in the garden?"

"I don't think that's a good idea," said Mrs Rhino. "If she runs around and gets hot, it will make her all itchy."

Mr Frog had made a huge lunch and Franklin and Ronnie were so hungry from running around outside that they ate and ate until they could hardly move.

"Can we go swimming in the river later?" asked Franklin.

"I don't see why not," said Mr Frog, "but you must let that great big lunch go down first! Would you like to go swimming too, Rachel?"

"I don't think that's a good idea," said Mrs Rhino. "The water will make her skin even more dry and itchy."

"Did you enjoy yourself today?" asked Mrs Frog as she put Franklin to bed.

"It was really good fun!" exclaimed Franklin. "I'm glad that Ronnie's moved in next door – he's my best friend!"

"That was quick," laughed Mrs Frog as she kissed Franklin goodnight.

Mr and Mrs Frog chatted as they did the washing up.

"Franklin and Ronnie seem to have really hit it off," said Mrs Frog. "But poor Rachel – her mother won't let her out of her sight."

"I know," said Mr Frog. "It can't be easy for her to be so itchy all the time."

The following week, Mrs Frog went shopping with her friend Mrs Hippo. When they had finished, they sat in a café and had a delicious water cabbage milk shake.

"Have you met Mrs Rhino yet?" asked Mrs Frog. "Her daughter is the same age as your Harriet. Perhaps they could play together."

"I don't think that's a good idea," exclaimed Mrs Hippo. "I've heard that she has an awful skin problem, and I wouldn't want Harriet to catch anything!"

"Oh, I don't think it's catching," said Mrs Frog.

"Well, I'd rather not take the chance," said Mrs Hippo, firmly.

15

"I don't want to go around to Ronnie's house again," announced Franklin at breakfast.

"But I thought he was your best friend," said Mrs Frog. "Have you fallen out already?"

"No," replied Franklin, "Ronnie's great, it's Rachel I don't like."

"Why ever not?" exclaimed Mrs Frog.

"Well, it's not that I don't *like* her," said Franklin slowly, "but looking at her makes me feel all funny. It's not just her face now, Mum – her legs and her tummy are all red and scaly, and she scratches and scratches all the time."

"That poor girl," thought Mrs Frog, and she decided to pay Mrs Rhino a visit.

Mrs Rhino made Mrs Frog a cup of tea.

"How's Rachel?" asked Mrs Frog, and was surprised to see Mrs Rhino's eyes fill with tears.

"She's so sore and itchy that she can't sleep at night," she cried. "And she should be starting

school soon but she says she won't go because the other animals will tease her. I just don't know what to do!"

Mrs Frog gave her new friend a tissue. "Let's take Rachel to see Doctor Spot," she said.

"How long has Rachel had problem skin?" asked Doctor Spot.

"Well, she's had dry skin since she was a baby," replied Mrs Rhino, "but it's much worse lately."

"What does it feel like, Rachel?" asked Doctor Spot.

"Itchy and hot and sore," said Rachel. "Mummy tells me not to scratch, but sometimes I just can't help it!"

"I'm not surprised," said Doctor Spot. "You have nasty case of eczema."

"What's eczema?" asked Rachel.

"Eczema is a dry skin condition," explained Doctor Spot. "The skin doesn't produce enough grease and loses water, so it becomes dry and itchy."

21

"How did I get eczema?" asked Rachel.

"There are many different types of eczema," said Doctor Spot. "I think you have something called atopic eczema, which is thought to be passed down through your family."

"But no one in our family has eczema!" exclaimed Mrs Rhino.

"Maybe not," said Doctor Spot, "but does anyone have asthma or hayfever? They are similar conditions."

"Why, yes," replied Mrs Rhino. "My brother has asthma."

"Can you make my eczema go away?" asked Rachel.

"Well, I can't make it go away completely," replied Doctor Spot, "but there are lots of things we can do to make you more comfortable."

23

"Your skin is short of grease and water, so we have to replace them with something called emollients," he continued. "There are all sorts of emollients – creams, lotions, ointments, bath oils and other things to wash with instead of soap. Which one you use depends on what your eczema is like. I am going to give you some cream to try, and some ointment for the creases on your neck and legs." Doctor Spot turned to Mrs Rhino. "Give her a bath every day and put bath oil in the water."

"Oh, I love baths," said Rachel gleefully. "Will I be able to go swimming now as well?"

"I don't think that's a good idea . . . " started Mrs Rhino, but Doctor Spot interrupted her.

"Swimming will be fine, Rachel," he said, "as long as you have an emollient on when you go in, and you put some more on when you come out."

25

Doctor Spot told Mrs Rhino how to sooth Rachel's eczema with a treatment called "wet wrapping".

That night, Mrs Hippo put ointment on Rachel's neck and legs and tummy where the eczema was worst, and she covered them with wet bandages. Then she put dry bandages over the top.

"Oh, that feels lovely," said Rachel. "It's all cool and I don't itch at all."

"You look just like an Egyptian Mummy," giggled Ronnie. "Can I be wrapped up too?"

"Well, maybe one dry bandage," said Mrs Rhino.

Rachel fell asleep as soon as she got into bed and she didn't wake up until the next morning. What a relief it was to have a good night's sleep! By the end of the summer holidays, Rachel's eczema was improving and she was looking forward to starting school.

"How was your first day at school?" asked Mrs Rhino.

"It was GREAT, Mum!" said Rachel. "We played games and had a story – and there's a really nice giraffe in my class called Gina, and she has eczema too! Can she come around to play after school?"

"Yes, that would be nice, dear," said Mrs Rhino. "Perhaps she could even stay the night if it's all right with her parents."

"I wonder if Gina has wet wraps at night?" said Rachel. Ronnie started grinning.

"What's so funny about that?" demanded Rachel.

"I was just wondering how many bandages it would take to wet wrap a giraffe's neck!" he giggled.

Parents' pages: Eczema

What are the symptoms?

- Dry, red, itchy, scaly skin, anywhere on the body
- Small blisters
- Weeping, swollen skin
- Persistent scratching of affected areas
- Irritability
- Darker or paler looking skin (in African-Caribbean and Asian children)

What should I do?

- Take your child to see your doctor

Will my doctor prescribe a medicine?

- Your doctor will advise you which emollients to use to soothe and soften the skin
- Your doctor may prescribe a topical steroid to reduce inflammation, or an antihistamine to help your child sleep
- Antibiotics may be useful if the skin has become infected

Will my child grow out of eczema?

- It's impossible to say. About 90% of children have outgrown eczema by the time they reach adulthood, although some may have drier than usual skin. Some people have it all their lives, in varying degrees of severity. The course of eczema cannot be predicted, but it bothers people less if they learn how to control it.

Doctor Spot says:

- Distract your child from itching as much as possible through play.
- Try not to tell your child to 'stop scratching'.
- Keep finger nails short and use scratch mittens at night.
- If your child gets hot, the itching will be worse. Make sure your child has plenty to drink in hot weather and always apply a sunblock in the sun. Don't overheat your home in the winter. Don't let children sit next to radiators or sunny windows.
- Tepid baths soothe the itching. Always add a medicinal bath oil and use soap substitutes.
- Wet wrapping can make your child more comfortable and stops scratching, but should not be used on infected skin.
- Atopic eczema is linked to allergens (things that cause an allergic reaction). Regular vacuuming, dusting with a damp cloth and using special anti-dust mite bedding can help. Pets with fur, hair or feathers can also aggravate eczema. If you have a pet, cut down its contact with your child and keep it out of the bedroom.
- Some complementary treatments such as homeopathy seem to have some success in managing eczema for some children, but should not be used at the same time as conventional medicine.
- Try not to prevent your child from joining in activities with other children. The eczema may flare up as a result, but it is best not to make them lead restricted lives.
- Remember, eczema may look unpleasant, but you cannot catch it from someone who has it.
- For further information on eczema, contact the National Eczema Society information line on 0870 241 3604, or visit their website: www.eczema.org .

Other titles in the series:

Harriet has Tonsillitis
ISBN: 1-902463-37-4
Harriet the Hippopotamus has a nasty case of tonsillitis at her best friend's birthday party. Luckily, Doctor Spot is at hand to make her feel better.

Mike has Chicken-pox
ISBN: 1-902463-38-2
Mike the Monkey comes out in spots and feels uncomfortably itchy. But he soon feels better when Doctor Spot prescribes a soothing lotion.

Lawrence has Nits
ISBN: 1-902463-90-0
Lawrence the Lion gets a shock when the barber finds nits in his mane. Luckily, Dr Spot's nurse can provide a remedy. Dr Spot visits Lawrence's school to tell the class about head lice and how to tackle them.

Charlie has Asthma
ISBN: 1-902463-68-4
Charlie the Cheetah finds he's always running out of breath. Doctor Spot tells him what's wrong and gives Charlie a special inhaler to help him breathe more easily.

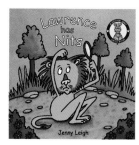

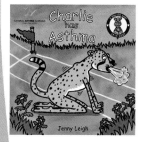

George has Meningitis
ISBN: 1-902463-91-9
George the Gorilla is feeling very ill. His sister, Gloria, remembers her school lesson about the tell-tale signs of meningitis, and gets her father to call in Doctor Spot without delay.

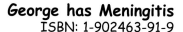